Ruby's Sleepover

For Suzy, love Mum — K. W.
To Miranda, lots and lots of love xx — M. L.

Barefoot Books
2067 Massachusetts Ave
Cambridge, MA 02140

Barefoot Books
29/30 Fitzroy Square
London, W1T 6LQ

First published in Great Britain by Barefoot Books, Ltd
and the United States of America by Barefoot Books, Inc. in 2012
This paperback edition first published in 2018

Graphic design by Judy Linard, London
Reproduction by B & P International, Hong Kong
Printed in China on 100% acid-free paper
This book was typeset in Triplex and Hoagie Infant
The illustrations were prepared in acrylic paints
and watercolor pencils

Paperback ISBN 978-1-84686-758-3

British Cataloguing-in-Publication Data: a catalogue record for this book
is available from the British Library

Library of Congress Cataloging-in-Publication Data is available under LCCN 2011031914

3 5 7 9 8 6 4

Ruby's Sleepover

Written by **Kathryn White**
Illustrated by **Miriam Latimer**

Barefoot Books
step inside a story

I'm sleeping with Mai in my tent tonight,
When the **moon** is full and the **stars** are bright.

We're both so excited!
We **whoop** and we **jump**,
Into the tent we **tumble** and **bump**.

One bag on this side, one bag on that,
Mai's brought her teddy
and I've brought my cat.

I open my bag up and show Mai my things:
My **egg**
and my **beans**
and my **magical rings**.

We nibble our snacks
and hear foxes bark.
Then we turn on our lights
to see in the **dark**.

The **moon** shines above us;

there's no one about.

We snuggle down deep

with our eyes peeking out.

I'm not at all nervous; I feel quite prepared.

"Don't worry," I say,

"there's no need to be scared."

But a **rumble** —

a **grumble!** —

roars loud down the street.

Mai grabs my arm and jumps to her feet.

I giggle and say, "A **giant** is near."

Mai screeches out,

"Don't let it in here!"

"I'll toss out these **beans**

so they'll grow up so high

That the **giant** can climb

to his home in the sky."

I hold out the beans and I give them a **shake**.

As the giant gets nearer I feel the earth **quake**.

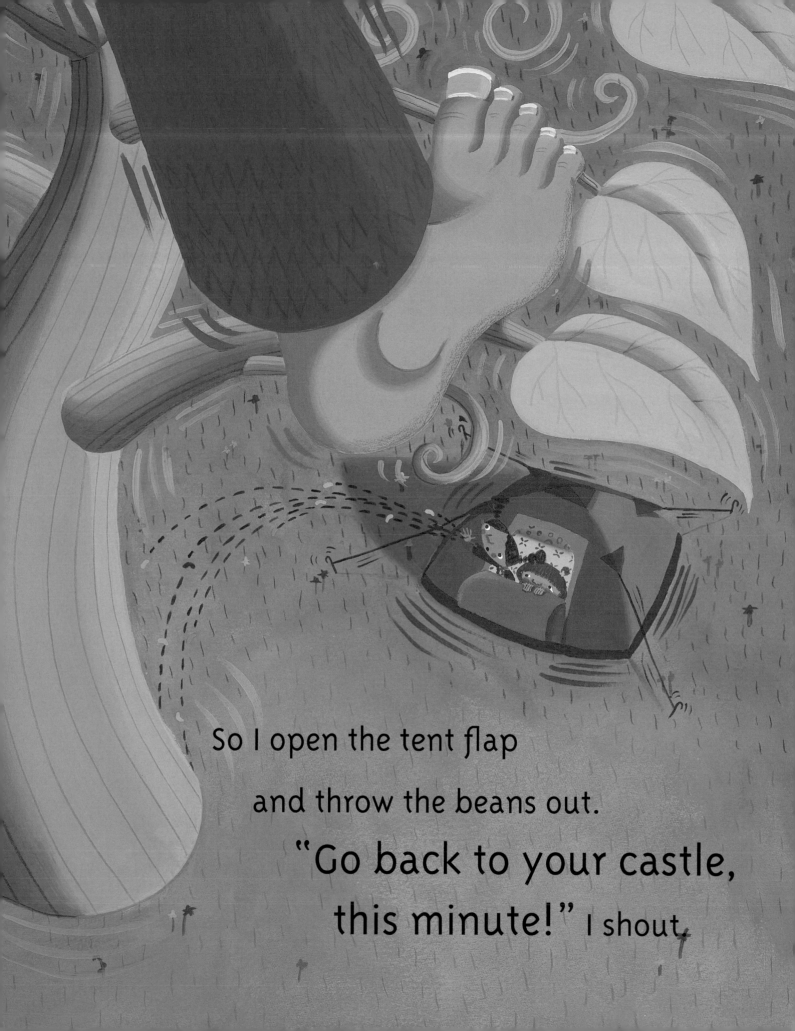

So I open the tent flap
and throw the beans out.
"Go back to your castle,
this minute!" I shout.

An owl **hoots** a warning from high in the trees. The tent starts to **rustle** and **shake** in the breeze.

"Did you see that shadow?"
Mai trembles in fright.
I whisper, "A **dragon** is coming tonight."

"And when it comes **huffing**
and **puffing** about,

Snorting out
flames from its
long purple snout,

I'll send it away on a **magical quest**:
It must carry this **egg** safely back to its nest."

So I open the tent flap and call to the sky,

"Here is your **dragon's egg**, take it and fly."

I take out my **rings** to keep danger at bay;

I slip one on my finger and give one to Mai.

We can't hear a sound now, not even a peep.

But we feel really brave as the world falls asleep.

Then Mai starts a story
her grandfather told,
Of swashbuckling **pirates**
all hunting for **gold**

With **magical ships** that sail from the **moon**.

I look up and say, "They'll be flying here soon."

"And they'll carry us off to scrub the decks clean.

They'll be **rotten** and **smelly**

and **nasty** and **mean**."

They're close to the tent now;

they're creeping around.

"**Shhh!**" I tell Mai.

"We must **not** make a sound."

But Mai is asleep,

with a sweet little **snore**.

And I really don't feel quite

as brave as before.

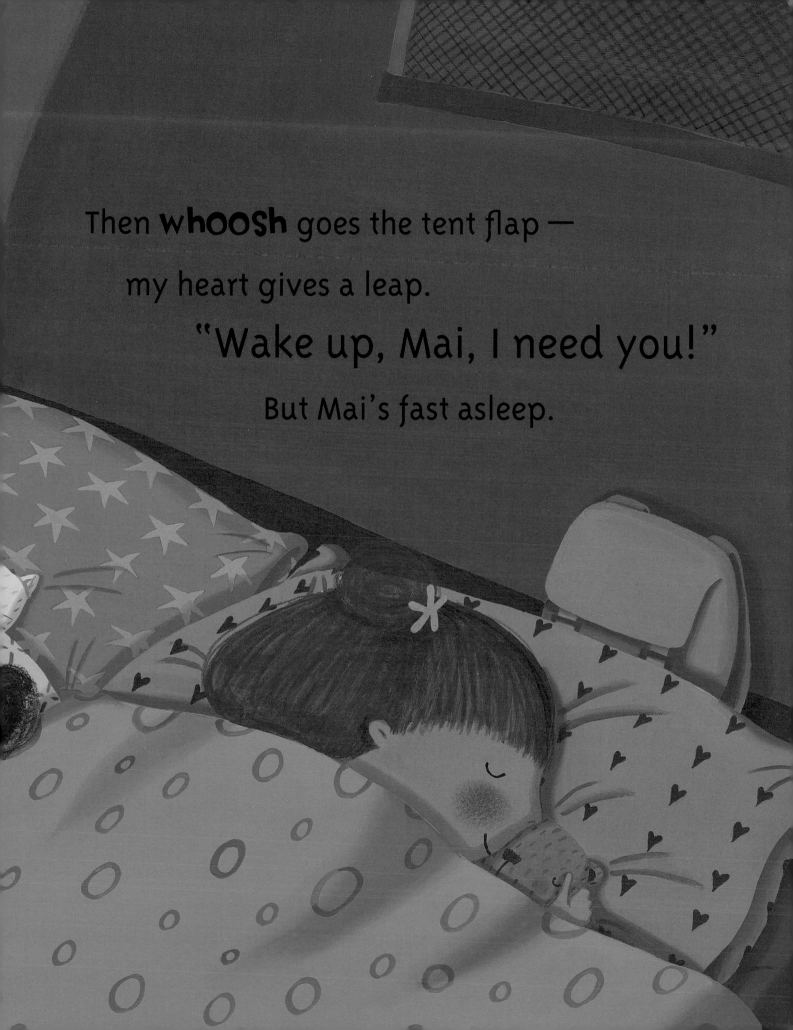

Then **whOOSh** goes the tent flap —

my heart gives a leap.

"Wake up, Mai, I need you!"

But Mai's fast asleep.

So I hold out my **ring**

and I scrunch up my eyes,

"Oh wind, take those **pirates**

back up to the skies.

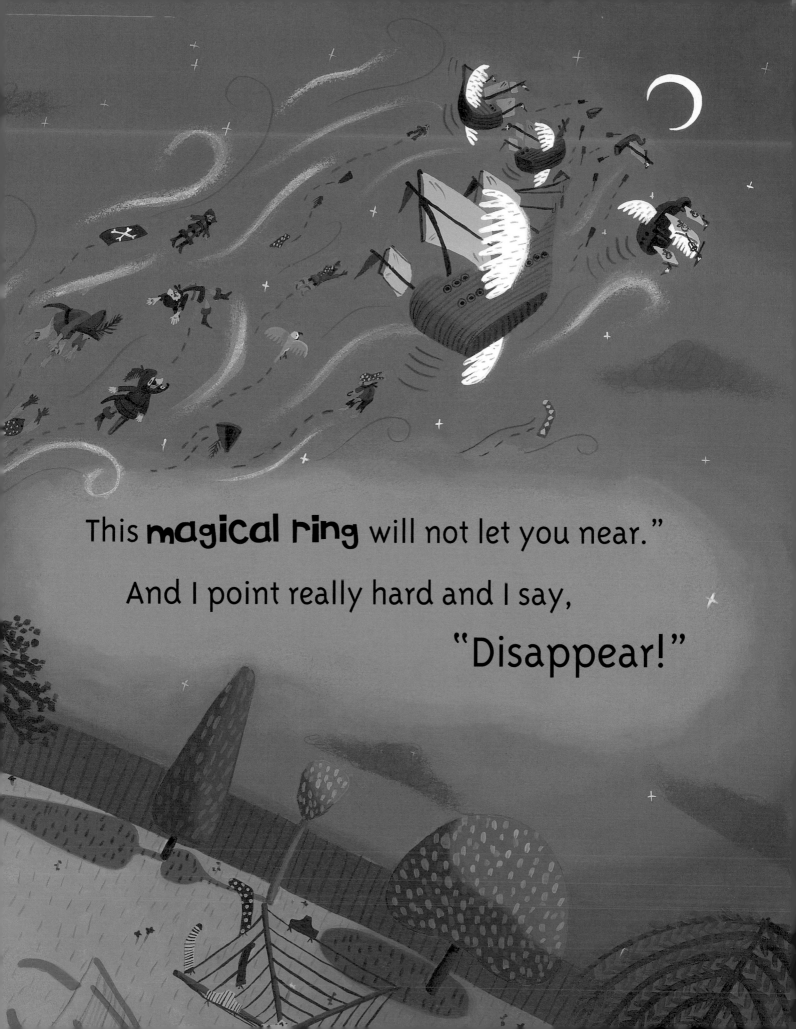

This **magical ring** will not let you near."

And I point really hard and I say,

"Disappear!"

The tent flap stops moving —

I hug my ring tight.

So **giants**

and **dragons**

and **pirates**,

"Goodnight!"